SOME DAYS

For Rosa, my mother

Previously published as *Hay Días* by Calibroscopio Ediciones in Argentina in 2012. Translated from Spanish by
Lawrence Schimel. First published in English by Amazon Crossing Kids in collaboration with Amazon Crossing in 2020.

Published by Amazon Crossing Kids, New York, in collaboration with Amazon Crossing
www.apub.com

Amazon, Amazon Crossing, and all related logos are trademarks of Amazon.com, Inc., or its affiliates.

ISBN-13: 9781542022514 (hardcover)
ISBN-10: 1542022517 (hardcover)

The illustrations were rendered in acrylic on paper.
Book design by Abby Dening
Printed in China

First Edition
1 3 5 7 9 10 8 6 4 2

SOME DAYS

Written and illustrated by
María Wernicke

Translated by
Lawrence Schimel

amazon**crossing kids**

Ma, I want to tell you something. . . .

In our yard, there's a passageway.

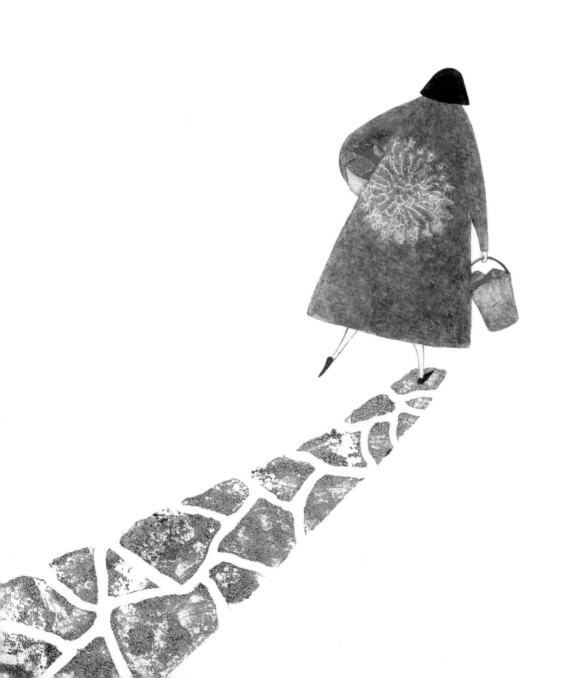

It's not a well, it's not a hollow in a tree.
And it doesn't have a door.

There are days when it's not there.

I would like it to always be there,
like today.

Because on the other side,

I've already learned how to swim.

And it's not cold,

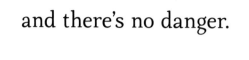

and there's no danger.

And nothing, nothing at all, can happen to you.

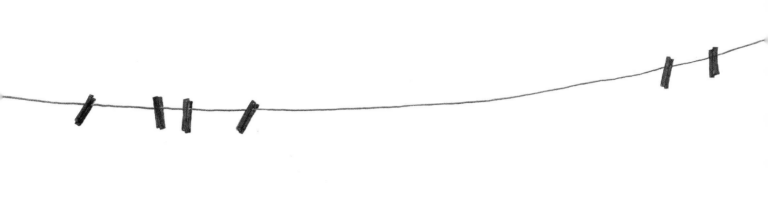

I would like it to always be there,

forever and ever.

There's something I want to tell you as well.

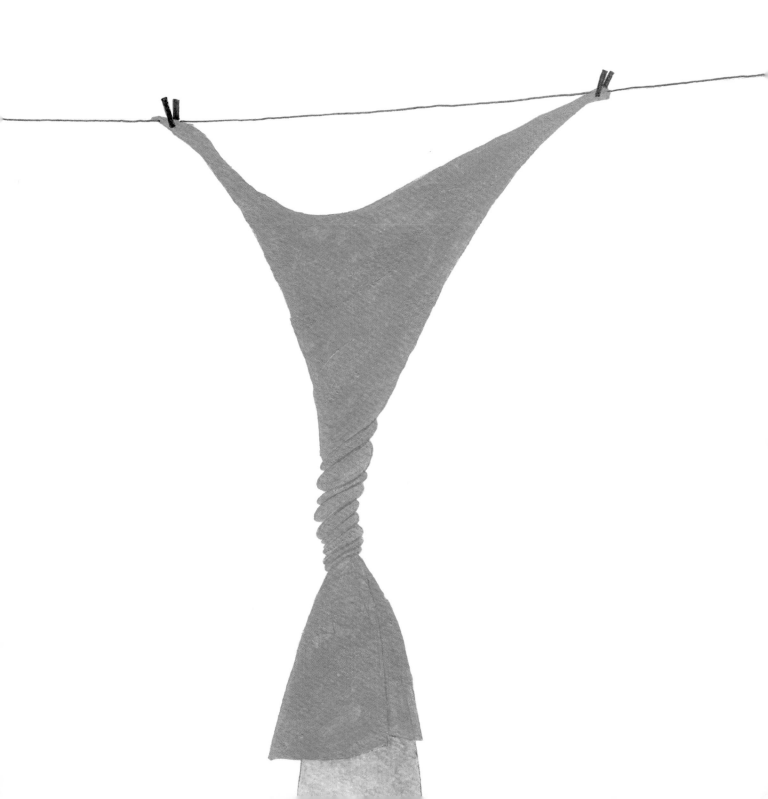

Although we may not always see it,

we can always go looking for it.

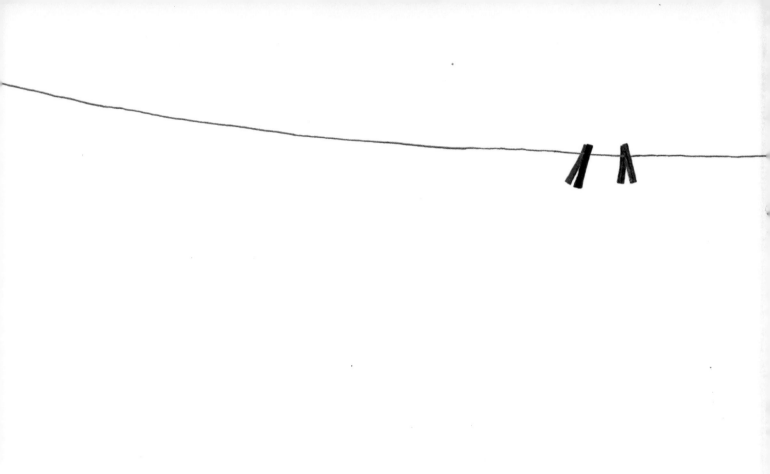